W9-BFM-668

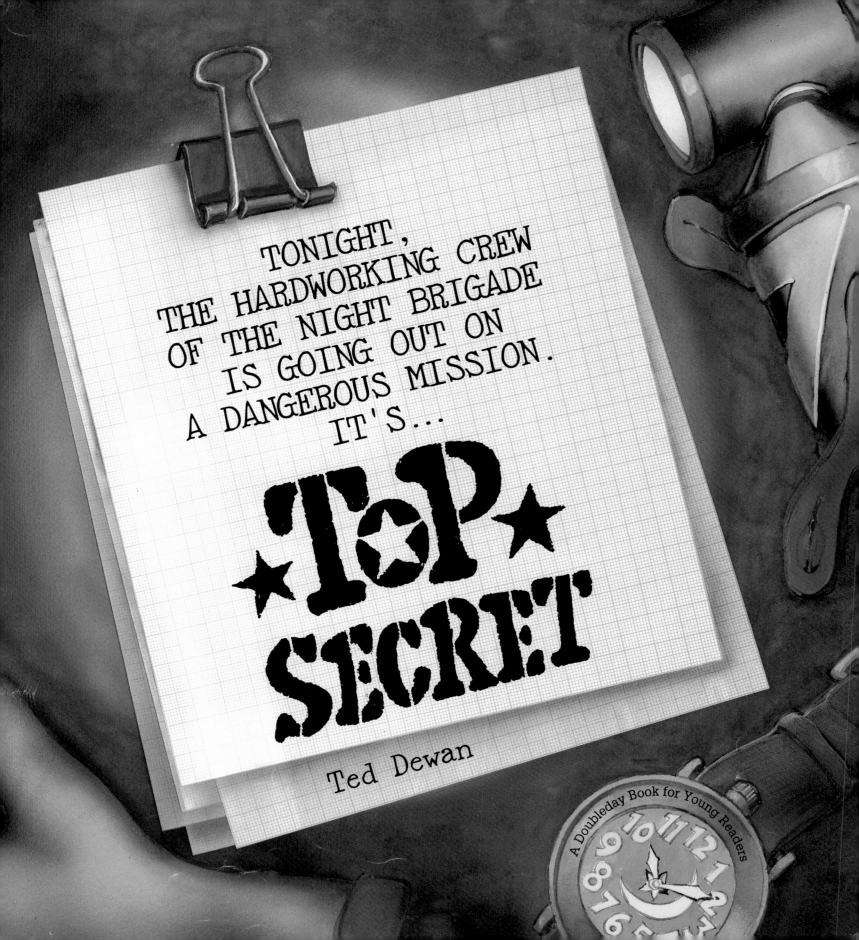

TONIGHT,
THE HARDWORKING CREW
OF THE NIGHT BRIGADE
IS GOING OUT ON
A DANGEROUS MISSION.
IT'S...

★ TOP ★
SECRET

Ted Dewan

A Doubleday Book for Young Readers

Can you keep a secret?
<u>Promise</u> not to tell, 'cause
this is a BIG secret.
First here's the crew of
the Night Brigade:

there's
Number 1,
the Captain...

...Number 2,
the Deputy...

...Number 3,
the
Navigator...

...Number 4,
the
Mechanic...

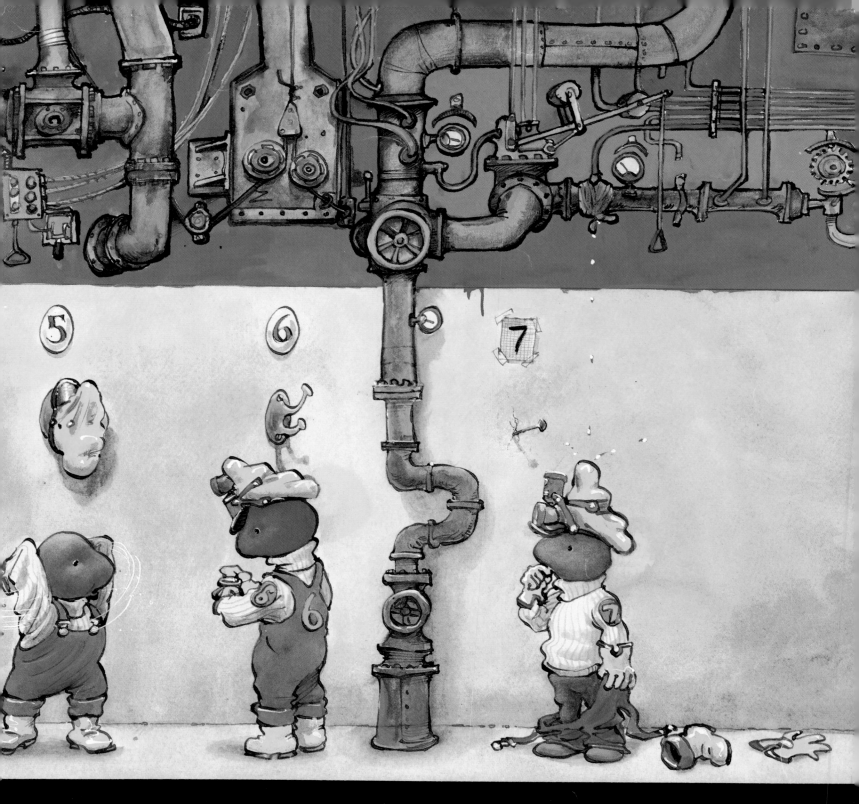

Number 5, ...Number 6, ...and me. I'm Number 7, the the and I joined the Night Muscle... Timekeeper... Brigade on Tuesday.

Being the new kid is not easy.

The crew boss me around a lot and call me 'Squirt'.

Everyone has their own Night Brigade wristwatch... except me,

'cause I'm the new kid.

ALL FOR ONE AND ONE FOR ALL
UNITED WE STAND DIVIDED WE FALL

YO!

...so the crew can ZIP in.

...like climbing inside to fasten the zip cable...

The new kid has to do all the dangerous work...

The wagon is built fast...

...wound up...

...and we're off.

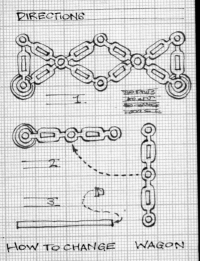

DIRECTIONS

HOW TO CHANGE WAGON

When we get to the big furry cliffs, we change the wagon

into the liff-climber.

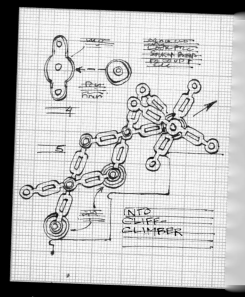

It's a tough
climb, but we
always make it
to the top.
Now we all go
dead quiet,
because here's
where the re
action
star

SHHH.

We're
going
into...

...The Slumber Zone.

In the Slumber Zone, the crew work together like well-oiled machinery...

...or ELSE.

Make a mistake in the <u>Zone</u>, and you're <u>squashed</u>.

We hoist
ourselves up
the lift...

...one
by one.

The suction cup sticks on here.

They use a candle to make hot air.

Wow!

It floats!

...to fetch the treasure.
It's the most beautiful tooth I've ever seen.
Wait... better not forget to leave this.

Just as I get out of the tunnel, the balloon starts sinking.
There's no time to waste.

The crew build quickly under the sinking balloon...
...and tie everything together to make...

...The Sky Buggy.

DIVIDED WE FALL! YO!

Remember, you <u>promised</u> to keep
our Mission a secret, so don't
tell anyone else, not even your
teddy bear. And the tooth? Sorry,
but we're not allowed to tell <u>anybody</u>
what we do with all the teeth...
not even <u>you</u>...

...it's TOP SECRET.

A Doubleday Book for Young Readers

Published by
Bantam Doubleday Dell Publishing Group, Inc.
1540 Broadway
New York, New York 10036

Doubleday and the portrayal of an anchor with a dolphin are trademarks of Bantam Doubleday Dell Publishing Group, Inc.

First American edition 1997

Originally published in the United Kingdom by Scholastic Ltd., 1996

Library of Congress Cataloging-in-Publication Data
Cataloging-in-Publication data is available from the U.S. Library of Congress.

ISBN: 0-385-32324-7

April 1997

Printed and bound in Hong Kong   10 9 8 7 6 5 4 3 2 1

For Helen